Rainy Day Picnic

by Jay Dale

illustrated by Nadia Ronquillo

"Oh, no!" said Rosie.
"It's raining outside."

"Oh, no!" said Cam.
"We cannot go to the park
for a picnic."

Mum looked out of the window.
Mummy looked
out of the window too.

"Oh, no," said Mum.
"The rain **is** coming down."

Rosie was not happy.
"The rain is no fun at all,"
she said.

"The rain **can** be fun!"

said Mummy.

"We can have a picnic inside.

It will be lots of fun."

"Yes!" said Cam.

"Let's have a picnic inside."

Rosie did not look happy.
"The rain is no fun at all,"
she said.
"It makes me sad!"

"Oh, Rosie," said Mummy.

"On a hot day,

you can go swimming.

On a snowy day,

you can play in the snow."

"And on a rainy day," said Mum,

"you can have a picnic inside!"

Rosie jumped up.

Cam jumped up too.

"I will get the picnic blanket," said Rosie.

"I will get the picnic basket," said Cam.

"Let's have a rainy day picnic," said Mum.

Rosie was very happy.
"A rainy day picnic
is lots of fun," she said.